LEGIT BALLERS

by

Eartha Simmons

Hello Readers

I am overly excited about this journey I am about to embark on.
This Book is my first of many. Hopefully you will take this ride
with me. I would like to thank first and foremost God for the
ability to stand upright when someone knocks me down. My
Pastor Mitchell and his Wife Joanne for continued support. My
mother, Marjorie, for birthing the gift because she is the real
writer in this family. My sister Tonya for her undying support
for me. My Children Kamaria, Tongeea, Marquise, and Miracle
for putting up with a little less attention these past few months.
My Cousins Shawn, Sharell, Kenneth, Derek and Deshaun for
believeing in me. Last but not least to Shades Up Inc. Charlie
Rose, Sweet Tea, Miss J and Juicy, You all are the bomb. This
bond we have created is awesome and I can't wait for things on
our agenda to come to pass. This is the first stepping stone. We
are well on our way.

This Book is Dedicated to:

Crystal Harris and Kenneth Harris

Simone (Earlier)

We can end this right now. To continue to live in this fucked up state of mind that you are the reason I am who I am is not what's happening <u>anymore</u>. If you are going to continue to throw shade my way, cover your eyes then playa, cause my light is going to shine like a diamond without your ass. I am done, and this time it's nothing you can do about it. So the fuck what you suggested I go back to school. So what I'm living a life that I never imagined would come to pass. And so the fuck what I have clothes that would make Kim Kardashian look like she shops at a rummage sale. Nigga, I earned this shit. Every last part of it. Think about it, Had I not took you up on your suggestion of going back to school to get my Business and financial degrees, how would your money be clean. Had I not showed you that investments were more than purchasing houses and cars, how thick you think that bank account would be. Now you want to question me about my whereabouts. Who I have my dealings with, and what I can and can't say to somebody. Don't call me and don't look for me. I need Space. And a lot of it. I'm tired of the drama and tired of the accusations. I'm a Boss. I don't work for you. I'm not your little employees so don't treat me as such. When you get your head out them other bitches pussy then maybe we can talk. But right now, Today, It's a rap. Catch me in the wind. Hopefully, it doesn't blow me too far away cause at this very moment It feels like a windstorm in this bitch, and I'm getting as far away as I can.

Still Simone

I keep playing the words I said to June over and over in my mind. I don't think I was wrong, but I may have over did it. It was some truth to his claims. I have always been smart, but upon meeting him and living a little of the street life, I had given up on school. But he encouraged me to go back. Make our money legitimate so that if anything ever happened to him, my living would still be lavish. But I was tired of the whole, "Girl I made you" cliché'. Naw nigga Roberta made me. I was one of the best accountants in The Chi, and I made moves that most didn't know was possible. I was also in business management, so our dirty money has been cleaned by the bucket loads. You would think that now we could live in peace and harmony but no. Ever since June had been able to relinquish most of his street duties to the up and comings in the streets, he has been stressing me the hell out. Where have you been? Where are you going? What time are you coming in? Who you going to be with? Ugggh....I was done. Now have I ever given him reason to think otherwise? Well maybe but that was the past, and we have moved on from that. I loved my man, but I refused to have a lie detector quiz every time I crossed our threshold. So I'm going to visit my buddy in Calumet City, and he should hope that after our turn up session I would be back, but for right now I need a breather.

As I pulled up behind Charmaine's 2017 Mercedes-Benz AMG G63, I began to get pumped. I so needed a drink. I just wanted June's ass to sweat a little. I wasn't going anywhere, but I needed him to know that I would not continue to put up with his accusations and nagging like he was a bitch. I loved his ass, But love didn't always make me bring my ass home I night. I mean yes I was a huge flirt, but I just liked the rush of it because these cookies belong to June. He just thought he knew that I was unfaithful because of a few sleazy texts or uneasy encounters in public but he had been the One and only man I had been with since the day I met him. I would never give him the satisfaction of knowing that though because his name rang supreme in the streets and even louder in the sheets. Hell, I had to put in work on these hoes to keep them away, but I knew I was the one that had his heart and deep down inside nothing else really mattered.

June

I promise you Simone is going to be the death of me. I was pounding the pavement when Chris hit me up and said that he wanted to go and have brunch with a nigga. I mean that's how we got down now. We had so much money from so many sources that we stepped out in Corthay shoes just because. No more Hoadies and White Palace we did Brunch at Cite' and had cocktails at Theory. We loved the life we lived. So once we ordered and got our food, we chopped it up in just casual conversation. I mean Chris and I was business partners, and longtime hustlers so it was good to catch up every now and then.

During the course of our conversation, I peeped this nigga Drake from Atlanta walking our way. I wondered what he was doing in town, but that was short lived when he stopped right at our table. Hey, fellas what's good in The Windy City. Chris answered and said you tell us, man; we can't call it. We all dapped up and I offered him a seat. He sat, and we breezed through a few Conversations. The One that caught my attention was how he said that he came to town because he was in business with one of Chi 'Towns finest accountants. Ms.Simone Savvy. He went on to say how she had cleared up a lot of things for him and how he wished that one day he could just bend her over her desk and show her just how much he thanked her. I raised an eyebrow but remained calm. He went on to say that she was a big flirt but never let him sniff her cookies. He licked his lips and said he only prays he can get a whiff of that big ass because she had it going on. I hit the table, startling Drake. Of course, Chris knew the deal but maybe it was now time I let Drake know. I went on to say through gritted teeth, Listen Drake; the possibility of that accountant letting you get a whiff is slim to none. Now out of respect for you and our business dealings, I'm going to give you a pass, but Simone Savvy is not up for a disrespectful ass conversation. That's my Bitch. You've been warned. Oh, my bad, I'm sorry, she told me she wasn't married. And I didn't see a ring on her finger. Aggravated I got up and said look Chris I'm going to catch you later and Drake good seeing you once again. Now upon leaving My City don't forget you have been warned.

I couldn't wait to talk to Simone's ass. I have told her over and over again about being overly nice to these niggas. She acts like this shit is sweet out here. She is continuing to disrespect our boundaries, and she knew what she was doing. I called her phone, and she answered, Hey babe. Don't fuckin Hey me. Excuse me, she answered, I replied you heard what the fuck I said. So who has ruffled your feathers today June? Maybe I should ask you who you are trying to let ruffle your feathers, Simone. Look I'm not gonna continue to tell your ass how to run your business. We have been through this too many times. All the flirtatious shit should be out the door. And since when did we relinquish the status of our relationship to niggas on the other side of the train tracks. You trying to let niggas know I haven't wifed you yet? Keep playing with me, and I'm going to clap your Mother fuckin' ears together. You are pushing it. She went on a rampage after my last statement. Look June. I am sick and tired of you trying to tell me what I should and shouldn't do. Simone if it wasn't for me your ass would still be some little church mouse singing the Lord's Prayer, waiting for someone who could afford a meal like I can, so don't go there with me. Really June, well guess what. We can end this right now. To continue to live in this fucked up state of mind that you are the reason I am who I am is not what's happening anymore. If you are going to continue to throw shade my way, cover your eyes then playa, cause my light is going to shine like a diamond without your ass. I am done, and this time it's nothing you can do about it. So the fuck what you suggested I go back to school. So what I'm living a life that I never imagined would come to pass. And so the fuck what I have clothes that would make Kim Kardashian look like she shops at a rummage sale. Nigga, I earned this shit. Every last part of it. Think about it, Had I not took you up on your suggestion of going back to school to get my Business and financial degrees, how would your money be clean. Had I not showed you that investments were more than purchasing houses and cars, how thick you think that bank account would be. Now you want to question me about my whereabouts. Who I have my dealings with, and what I can and can't say to somebody. Don't call me and don't look for me. I need Space. And a lot of it. I'm tired of the drama and tired of the accusations. I'm a Boss. I don't work for you. I'm not your little employees so don't treat me as such. When you get your head out them other bitches pussy then maybe we can talk. But right now, Today, It's a rap. Catch me in the wind. Hopefully, it doesn't blow me too far away cause at this very moment It feels like a windstorm in this bitch, and I'm getting as far away as I can.

I hung up on her ass. She knew she had a nigga's heart, but for the life of me, I couldn't understand why bitches needed a ring a piece of paper to solidify that shit. When I catch her ass up today, I'm going to fuck her up.

Simone

Hey Boo, I said to Charmaine as she stepped out in her new Alexander McQueen Jumpsuit shorts and Some Brunello Cucinelli Thong sandals. Hair 22 inches with a light, bouncy curl and face beat to the Gods as always. Bitches hated us. But as long as the hate was real we were going to ride the wave. I joined her in her driveway with my Chloe' pleated back out maxi that was flowing with the wind and my Rene Caovilla flat sandals. This was the life, and we were definitely living it. We hugged, and I told her we were riding the Benz because I felt a night of too much to drink and would not be driving home. She laughed, and we headed onto the expressway.

We just wanted to do something local today, so we would just chill at Tilly's Bar and Grill. It was overly crowded tonight because one of the local hustlers was celebrating his Birthday. We made our way to the bar and began our night. As we were sipping and talking I felt someone breathing down my neck which caused me to turn around with a scowl on my face. Can I help you? "Actually, you have helped me just by gracing your presence in my establishment." The tall cup of Mocha said. Hi,

I'm Martell, and you are? Simone. Simone Savvy, I responded. Well Hello, Ms. Savvy, I'm Martell Jerrod, and I was wondering if you will allow me to pick up your bar tab. Well, Umm…. "That won't be necessary, and by the way, it's Mrs. Savvy stated the deep voice is standing behind Mr. Martell which I knew belonged to June. Damn!!!! Always cramping my style I said to myself. Oh, I apologize June, How are you these days. I'm Good Martell and how is your wife, Janet. Oh… Ummm she is good. I was just noticing this beautiful young lady who looked out of place, and I had no Idea that was you. She must have lost her wedding band….He said sarcastically. June frowned and said… No, it's being upgraded as we speak, but it was good seeing you and be sure to give my regards to Janet. Will do Martell said as he turned to walk away.

June leaned in and whispered in my ear. I had Moonie to pick up your car and take it home, Chris is on his way to get ya girl, so I'm going to say this once so please don't make me repeat it. Get your Shit. Meet me in my Aston Martin out front. Make a scene, and it's your ass. The tab is paid. Now make nice and give you man a kiss. Ha…. I laughed. I turned told Charmaine I was out of there and couldn't wait to get in the car so I could rip

June a new Asshole.

June

I kissed Charmaine on the jaw and proceeded to the front of the club where I noticed that punk Rell was Tossing it up like he didn't owe a nigga 50 G's. I made a mental note to text and let Chris know he was there and possibly collect that debt if it didn't Put Charmaine in harm's way. We never get dirty around our family, but sometimes you have to do what you have to do.

After sending that text, I got in my car and instantly held up my hand to let Simone know that I didn't want to hear shit. Just sit back and enjoy the ride I told her. I knew she was pissed and feeling some type of way, but we have never been in a place where we argued this much. I looked at her on the verge of tears and said, baby, what's wrong? Nothing, I'm just tired. It's been 9 Years June. I love you; you love me. We live together, eat together, Sleep together and make Power Moves together. You do want to marry me right? At this point, I knew it was some explaining I had to do. I pulled my car over and turned the inside lights on in the car and held my baby's face and said look, Simone, You are the very air I breathe. I would take a bullet for you right now. I just don't want you to regret being with me. I have never had anyone be by my side as you are. I love you, but I'm afraid that I will lose you.

Simone

As I sat in Junes car listening to him pour his heart out, I could not believe that he thought I would leave him. I Reached for his hand and pulled myself over the middle barrier to straddle him. Baby, I will never leave you. I may be spoiled and like to get my way, but you are who I want. Nothing else compares to what we have. I need you to know that. I wiped the tears from his ever and began to kiss hips lips gently. As he slid his tongue in my mouth, I could feel his bulge becoming a steel bat under my wetness. I hit the interior light so that if anyone drove pass, they would not notice what was about to take place. Since I wasn't wearing any panties, I just decided to reach down and allow him to enter the split that was now dripping wet. We gasped together as he entered my wetness; I rode his shaft straight into ecstasy. We both let out a big sigh because when we get passionate like that, it seems like we cum so quick. Satisfied I grabbed a wet wipe out of the glove compartment and cleaned him off and myself as well. I love you June Savvy, and he said I love you Simone Savvy. I smiled. And yes I know that I carry his last name even though we are not married but it was for business purposes. I love June but would be lying if I said I

didn't want to make it official.

June

I love Simone with all my heart. A nigga got to get it together though before I lose her. I'm driving looking at her as she lightly snores in my passenger seat. Damn! I have to fix this tonight. She deserves the world for riding with a nigga this long. I pulled out my phone to text Chris and let him know that I was headed to Vegas and him and Charmaine needed to meet us there to witness our nuptials.

When my baby wakes up, she is going to be so happy. It's time to make an honest woman out of Simone Richardson. Now she can wear Savvy with Pride. I tuned the radio to my Satellite R and B station and cruised towards Vegas. I was able to put some things in motion while Simone was sleeping.

I was able to get my private jet to get Charmaine and Chris from O'Hare Airport. They would stop at Midway airport private strip to get Simone's' Mother, Ms. Roberta, and then head here. Luckily there was a fashion event on the strip of Vegas because my contacts told me Vera Wang was in town so she could pull off a miracle for me. Once we all get there, Chris and I would handle some business in the city while the girls shop

for necessities and get ready for the wedding of the century.

Chris

June is finally making an honest woman out of my girl. I am so happy that June was finally going to step up to the plate. I know it's been hard knowing that they have been together nine years without a commitment, and I met her girl, Charmaine, at the same time, and we were married a year later. Either way, the time was now. I looked over on the other side of my California King Size bed and saw the most amazing woman lightly turning in her sleep. I thanked God every day for this one.

Charmaine, you need to wake up, I said as I pulled the sheets off her glistening body. She turned over and looked at the clock and said, really babe it's 3:00 am in the morning. Why are you breaking my sleep you know I have to open the boutique by 9. Then I leaned down and kissed the back of her shoulder and whispered you need to tell your employees you will be off for about a week because we have urgent business to attend to and we need to be gone in like 20 mins. Once I said that she jumped up like clockwork. She was my Ride or Die. She got in the shower with no questions asked. Once she returned to our room, she asked me should she take her piece or was she just the driver today. I let out a small smirk, and she looked confused. I had turned my baby into a Goon. I told her no baby the business is in Vegas and June has the Jet picking us up from O'Hare. She looked disappointed, but I smacked her on the ass and told her to calm down lil' killa.

Charmaine

Really? I could have kicked Chris's ass when he woke me up having me think we had to put a move on somebody. It wasn't funny to me. He knows that I'm about that life so when he needs me I'm right there. Now his ass taking a Shower and for the life of me I wondered why we were going to Vegas at 3 am in the morning, and why were we going in the Private Jet for that matter. Oh well, when he said for me not to pack and I can shop when I got there was explanation enough for me. I made a few calls and Texts to secure our businesses would run smoothly with the quick change in rotation.

Once Chris got out of the shower he stood in the doorway of the bathroom dripping wet. Now if he was rushing me then why would he stand there with my Ice Cream Bar pointing directly to me? He knows that I could not resist that. So I didn't. He said, No baby we have to go, I said 3 minutes, and he couldn't protest because I had already made his shaft play hide and seek in my mouth. Massaging his balls and making all 12 of his inches disappear had him going crazy he was trying to hold on to the wall to keep from falling. I Spit, sucked, and slurped for like 2 minutes, and I was now swallowing all of his children. He was so weak now. The only thing he could say was damn! Come on baby we have to go Chris said. So as he cleaned himself and got dressed he explained the reasoning behind this trip and I got overly excited. OMG, I am so happy for Simone. She had wanted this. And now my friend would get her desire to be the Mrs. Simone Savvy Fulfilled. This wedding is going to be epic.

Chris

Okay, wheels up. We will make a quick stop through Midway to get Roberta then Vegas here we come. This would be good timing though because once I had a casual conversation with that nigga Rell last night about that money he owed I can put June up on our next move in collecting that payment. When I got to the club, I saw Rell before Charmaine so I figured I would have a drink and casual conversation. Once I got over to VIP where he was sitting, I had the waitress grace us with a bottle of Remy Martin King Louis. I mean I might as well enjoy my drink just in case I had to murk this Nigga. I mean 50 G's wasn't a lot of money to June or me, but the principal behind it was law. Once the bottle arrived, I excused his entourage. I sipped on my glass and proceeded to tell him why I was paying him a visit. I made sure that he saw the Glock under my blazer. I sat my glass down and said, look, we both know why I'm here. My wife is in here so I would hate to have to make a scene. Just let me know when we should expect payment of that loan that you are three months late. Now be wise before you answer. Maybe you think we some punks because we haven't stepped to you, but we love to give the benefit of the doubt. However, at this point, your grace period has ended. Now pay up, or this will be your last taste of the good stuff. He looked at me and held his head down and tried to explain the issue. Look, Chris, I have no issue with giving yawl those racks, honestly until last week I thought that debt was cleared. Once I found out there was deceit amongst my men and a few debts hadn't been paid I put my best men on top of it. I sent my guy Bolo to clear those debts, but he never returned. Now my men have just reported back to me that this nigga is set up in Vegas and living like he can't be found. I'm scheduled to fly out there next week so that I can infiltrate his program. Once I'm back, my debt will be cleared up with you and June. As soon as I was about to dead this nigga I saw my beautiful wife looking my way and finding my presence invading hers. So quietly I got up, told him to enjoy the bottle, and I look forward to the recoupment of 150 g's because the late fees are adding up daily. Now that we will be in Vegas I got a whole new agenda for collections, and it may just be the best mini vacation of my life.

Ms. Roberta

What happens in Vegas will stay in Vegas baby, I said to myself while preparing to board June's private Jet. He called and said Momma don't pack anything. Just bring your ID's and purse. He didn't have to tell me twice. He was finally going to do it. Simone is my one and only child. He father was killed in an accident before she was born. I had raised her well and trusted her decisions. Though I didn't agree with all the ends and outs of Junes business dealings, he had begun to get farther and farther out of the game. He was a good man though. He was humble, and he made my daughter happy. Now, of course, the road was bumpy, but sometimes you can't help who you love.

June was raised in various foster homes and began dealing drugs at the tender age of 12. He met Chris in the last orphanage, and they have been inseparable ever since. I knew about both of their upbringings and current lifestyles because honey Ms. Roberta is nosey. Laugh all you want, but when the heat reigns down, you need to know where the force is coming from. June had been planning on giving Simone the wedding of her dreams next year, but he said he was ready, right now, today. I grabbed the 14K White Solid Gold Diamond Engagement Ring with Blue and Yellow Diamonds 13.71 Carats, Created by Mr. Harry Winston, that June had purchased maybe a year ago. Yes, I have been in on it for the longest, but one thing I have told Simone and I try to pass onto other young women. When a man isn't ready, he isn't ready. Wait until he's ready and if the wait is not what you are willing to do then move on.

Simone

Jeesh….It seems like I have been sleeping forever. Um, babe where are we and why are we still driving, I asked while we were passing what looked like desert land. June looked at me and smiled and said Awe baby you looked so peaceful sleeping that I just decided to take a ride. I then looked at the clock and said, I have been sleeping in the car this long, and I have a client in 20 minutes. June looked back with a smile once again and said, I rescheduled your clients for the next ten days, I have Moonie running the front offices, and I gave your secretary some much needed time off. I just wanted to drive around the world and stare at your pretty face. Is that a problem? Awe babe it's not a problem, but I don't have any clothes, shoes or underwear. How could you not let me pack? He looked at me once again and smiled and said well we are not that far from Las Vegas; I feel like gambling, so you can go shopping. What do you think? I grabbed his face and smiled and said I love you, babe.

I sat back and let the slight wind blow through the windows and thought to myself there are women that would kill for a man like this. I had decided right then and there that I would no longer nag him about marriage. I would let it happen naturally and just enjoy the lovely life that I had been blessed to live. I decided to pull out my phone to call my mother and let her know about my sudden trip, but my phone was dead. I asked June for his, and he asked who I was calling, and I told him, and he said no need he already informed her, Charmaine and Chris. I looked at him and said you have been very busy while I was asleep, haven't you? He replied that I wouldn't even know the half.

I allowed myself to lean back in relaxation mode. I noticed Junes Text message notification rang and he looked at it with a scowl and put his phone back down, Note to self, Check that message as soon as possible, but until then let me enjoy this ride.

June

Simone has no Idea of the plans I have in store for her. I want to give this girl the world. But just when you have plans for eternity somebody is always working against you. Now that I have put it in my mind that this is going to happen I will have to have a long sit down with my boo and explain some things to her. Although most of my history I've already explained to Ms. Roberta, there are some situations that are now trying to unfold.

My sister has been trying to contact me about my mom for over a month. I haven't ignored her, but I haven't given it much thought. My mom gave me up at five because she needed to live her life. After going from foster home to foster home, I finally decided to just make it on my own. Once Chris and I met we vowed to be brothers for life and build us an empire. That's exactly what we had done.

Never having anything as children afforded us with the opportunity of investing, instead of flashing. See we were true gangsters. But we moved in silence. It's not often that cats like us survived the game, but we were doing one hell of a job.

As I glanced over at Simone once again, she had drifted into a nap. Man, I love this girl. I just hope she is still willing after learning about some baggage in my life that I haven't unpacked yet.

Chris

MGM Grand was like a home away from home with me. I was prepared to go to my usual Penthouse suite when the concierge informed me that Mr. Savvy had already copped the Skyline Strip View Loft Suite. This was immaculate. June is always going above and beyond, but he knows I pay my way. I made a mental note to remove the charges from him and take care of it myself upon checkout. It would be one of their wedding gifts from me. Once we arrived at the hotel, Ms. Roberta hit the slots. She said to call my Cell when my baby arrives. I told her ok. She gave me a hug and whispered now get your ass up in that room and make some babies. I laughed. She had a funny way of doing things, but I loved her like she was my mother. I definitely was going to take her up on her offer.

Charmaine had gone and got some necessities and was now in the shower. She wasn't going to do any major shopping until Simone arrived. I was lying in bed thinking about where we come from and how we operated now. I wasn't perfect, but I thanked God for everything. I glanced behind me and noticed Charmaine looking my way. It's like every time we are together the physical attraction grows even stronger. I don't know if I believed in that soulmate shit, but she was definitely made for me. It was like I felt every urge in her body as she felt mine. I stood up, and our lips met. As our tongues begin to intertwine, I felt the warmth of her split. She was dripping wet. I was hard as a rock. I lifted her off the floor and put her back on the wall while she wrapped her legs around me and let my manhood enter her wetness. Damn baby this pussy so wet, I told Charmaine. She continued to let me take her there. I turned her around and placed her on the bed because I wanted to hit them guts. She began to scream, baby I'm about to cum. I pulled out and laid on the bed so she could ride this dick. OMG, she was working today. I had to grab her hips to slow down her pace cause I was about to release an army of seeds. She knew it, so she sped up her pace, and we collapsed as we became one in euphoric pleasures.

I got up to clean myself and came out of the bathroom to find Charmaine slightly snoring in the fetal position on the bed. I took the warm cloth to clean her and gave her a kiss on the forehead. While she was sleeping, I could hit up a few of my connects and see who this Bolo character was and what relevance he held here so I could put my plan in order.

Ms. Roberta

I've been playing these Slot Machines since we've arrived at the hotel. My blackjack game is nasty, so I'm sticking with what I know. As I look around this Casino, I notice a lot of meat that makes Stella want to get her groove back. Now don't get it twisted I could hang with the best of them. Baby, momma is thick in all the right places, and my sex game keeps the bills paid in advance. I was a savage honey and being in Vegas made me want to bring the beast out.

I kept noticing this tall glass of Carmel Latte with Dreads so neat and long looking my way licking his bottom lip. I had to check my panties just from what I was thinking. Ok, now I know what y 'all thinking but Ms. Roberta loves them young as long as they paying like they laying. Shit, I'm not looking for a husband just a little fun every now and then. I closed my eyes and wondered what he tasted like. As soon as I opened my eyes my latte was right in front of me.

Well look what has graced my presence with all this beauty, he said. What's your name ma? I'm Roberta, and you are? I asked as I took in his Balmain jean fit and his Ferragamo

Loafers. Brian, he said. But you can call me Bolo. I looked up at him and noticed this desire in his eyes and asked him was there something I can help him with. He said I was wondering if you will join me at the bar for a drink. I told him well maybe you can just grab a seat at this machine and entertain me while I continue to play. He never hesitated and was a bit mature for what I thought his age to be. So being me I flat out asked, So Brian, how old are you? He responded and said 29. I laughed as I asked him why are you over here with me I'm sure its other eye candy for you in your age group. He smiled and said well I live in Vegas, and none of these women surprise me. I've been there and done that. I like stability in my life, and it looks like you can offer that. I've never been into the girls around my age because all they see is status and money. I don't mind spending, but I like to invest where there is a return. I'm wise for my years, so usually, I go for the more seasoned women. So someone in their 40's doesn't scare me. Licking his bottom lip, I said well maybe someone who's 57 would. His eyes popped, and he said; now I know I have to have you. You are absolutely beautiful for your age. I said thank you. He looked at his watch and checked his surroundings and then stood up and said call me whenever you get some free time and handed me his card. I looked at him make his exit with a few men in front and behind him, and I couldn't help but think what Mr. Bolo could add to this vacation. I guess we will see.

June

Okay, baby, we are here, let's get up to the room shower and then you can go shopping. Simone was taking in the scenery. She loved the hustle and bustle of Vegas but had no idea what this trip really about to change our lives forever. When we arrived at the suite, Simone gasped and said Oh wow for a short stay babe this is beautiful. Once she got inside, she took in the ambiance and then heard a noise upstairs in one of the rooms.

She looked up and saw Charmaine and screamed and said what are you doing here? Charmaine said well we heard you guys were stopping through Vegas, so we decided to pop up and enjoy as well. I stopped and got some personals so we can go shopping when you are done showering. By the way June, Chris is in the den she yelled as they walked off gossiping. It's funny that Charmaine was sticking to the secretive plan we all had in motion, but I know once she sees her mom the suspicions are going to go through the roof. I looked in on Chris, and he got up, and we dapped it up. I asked how was the flight he said lovely. He informed me that Ms. Roberta was down in the casino and that he had done a little research on this guy Rell said ran off with our money.

I decided to go ahead and take a shower so that we could get down to business. It looks like I'm going to have my work cut out for me. See what Rell didn't know is that we would investigate on this end. Possibly recoup what was taken and then some, and then still collect on the debt from him because this was a personal loan, not a let me send someone else to take care of this debt. He should have made sure it was handled and if not there should have been words to Chris or me as to why. It's not the money. It's the Principal. My number one rule in these streets, once you let them think they can walk all over you ,they will continue to do it. That's not a part of our empire. Now it's time to make some people believers.

Simone

This was so nice that Chris and Charmaine could join us for a few days. June is full of surprises. I am in total shock with how he planned this whole mini-vacation, drive around the world ordeal, but I'm glad he did. I needed it. I can't wait to hit the designers out here. Charmaine said that we needed to see her friend about some custom made outfits first so after that its shop till we drop. While we are gone, I guess we can let the boys be boys.

Charmaine has done most of the shopping for the necessities already and grabbed me a nice little jumpsuit to throw on for now. Once I step out of the shower, I noticed June had just done the same. My baby was chiseled from head to toe. I so love this man. It's crazy how we got together, but everything happens for a reason I guess.

(Reminiscing)

Charmaine and I had been out for lunch at Coopers Hawk, and we noticed what seemed to be like a business meeting going on in the back of the restaurant. I loved to see black men dressed to the nines, smelling good, and looking like they were handling business. I walked to the ladies' room, and this Husky voice said, you need some help? I stopped and said, excuse me, I'm not sure what you are asking? And the whole table erupted into laughter. He then bashfully shook his head and said what's your name? I responded, Simone. And yours? June, June Savvy. Ok, Mr. Savvy it was nice meeting you. I hope you have a great day I said as I tried to walk off. He grabbed my arm and said is it possible that we could talk over cocktails. I answered and said, well let me go to the ladies room, then once I'm done I will talk it over with my girl and if she's ok with it and then you can join me at my table. Deal? He said deal.

Once back to my table I asked Charmaine, and she said it was fine as long as he brought his associate sitting beside him with him she had no problem. I motioned for him to come over and his buddy came along anyway, so there was no need to ask about him. He was so polite. He came over and introduced himself as Chris. Nice looking I thought but definitely not my type. He was a pretty boy and June was handsome as well, but he had that rough edge I loved. So we sat, ordered cocktails, talked, laughed and realized it had been hours. We were all in disbelief how the time had flown. We all made plans to meet up that night at Kryptonite to continue our introductory phases. As we proceeded to get up and leave the restaurant, we asked for the bill, but the bill had been paid, and we didn't even have numbers to contact our new found friends.

So we went to Charmaine's and talked about these two young men and had already declared that they were hustlers trying to come off legit. We were daredevils though so we were down. We were getting dressed for the night and headed on our way. After exiting Lower Wacker Drive, we pulled up in front of the club. The line was ridiculous. We were met by the Clubs security, and he asked for Our ID's at first why would he come to the end of the line and ask us I thought but then again ok. Upon looking at our ID's, he escorted us out the line and had security take us to VIP.

There awaited June and Chris in this secluded area of VIP. Two bottles of Armand de Brignac Ace of Spades Rose Champaign was on chill, and now it was time to enjoy the night. It was like we had been with them forever. We were hanging, enjoying the scenery, and enjoying the company.

While we were mid-conversation, a young man walked up looking drunk and disturbed. I noticed as he staggered and flopped down on the couch to talk to Chris that he wasn't drunk at all, So I alerted Charmaine by text, and we just paid close attention. He leaned over to Chris while reaching inside his coat. Chis looked up to notice their security was otherwise occupied and not nearby. Charmaine and I locked eyes. June was so into me that he had not noticed this guy pull out his banger and up it on Chris. Charmaine's trained eye shot to me while I Placed my Colt Mustang XSP directly to his temple which made him drop his pistol and then he saw Charmaine pointing his pistol directly at him. At this point, Chris and June were able to regain composure and have him taken care of, and Charmaine and I could bask in the fact that we almost had a situation and as always we stayed on point. Once cleared Chris and June made it back to VIP and motioned that they were ready to go and for us to exit with them. June said that we should get in the truck that was waiting and wait for them to arrive at his house. I told him that we drove and he put his hand up as if he didn't want to hear any explanations and we just went to the truck.

Once we arrived at this gorgeous Mini Mansion blocked off in Olympia Fields our mouths dropped. Like we weren't living shabby, but this was a step above the rest. The Driver pulled into the gate and drove maybe about a 1/2 of a mile until we got to the front of this massive space. We got out and was greeted by a woman that already knew who we were. She escorted us in and asked us to retire on the patio by the water, and Mr. Savvy would be there soon. There was a full bar for our enjoyment and also finger foods. Charmaine and I chatted and drank until we saw them enter a short time after we arrived.

They sat down, and Chris immediately began to thank us for our assistance. June chimed in and said that in all honesty, we had knocked them off their square. They had no intention of *trouble at a place that they really didn't frequent, but you can never be too sure. They were very sorry and never intended on putting us in harm's way. Then all of a sudden Chris began to laugh, and June joined in and said so What yall' a part of some type of Girl Mafia or something? I answered and told them, no, but we did know how to take care of ourselves because our momma didn't raise any fools and from that point, up until now we have had an unbreakable bond. Sure we've had our ups and downs, but we are still on cloud nine.*

Ms. Roberta

So I have finally made it up to this suite. I have won about three stacks, and now I need to stash it. Now my money was my money, and this was not my vacation, so I did not need my money. Once I got to my room, I noticed June had made it. I asked Chris where the girls were and he said shopping. He said he told Charmaine to pick up me some items because he knew I didn't want to walk up and down that strip. And he knew correctly.

I walked in and nudged June, and he woke up. Gave me a hug and a kiss on the jaw and said thanks mom for coming. I told him he knew I would not have missed it for the world. I gave him the box with the ring, and he smiled. Looked like he was going to tear up, but I just grabbed his hand and said, son its time.

I would not just give my baby girl to anyone. Now June was a little rough around the edges but hell so was Simone. I raised her that way. Sometimes I hate how rough she was but deep down inside they were both puppies, and they were made for each other.

I got up to make my way to my room, and Chris asked how the tables were looking, and I told him they were tight. He knew that meant I had hit a few times. I told him I was down there getting my groove on. Then I turned to look at him, and June standing in the hallway stuck looking at me out the side of their necks. What yall looking at me like that for? Shit yall already know how I get down. They laughed and held they head down. I told them I think I ran up on a little rich youngster that I think by the time we leave I will at least have my Mortgage and two car payments on lock. June said he just don't know what he is going to do with me. I laughed and went to the bathroom so that I could shower. Chris is not so accepting. He told me I need to sit my ass down and find me a nice man on Social Security and grow old with him. I hollered through the bathroom door, and what fun would that be. Don't get it twisted; I had it going on. Hell, why you think June sprung on the Pussy I brought in this world. Cause she gets it from her momma. Now leave me the hell alone so I can take a shower.

Chris

That damn Ms. Roberta never fails for bringing excitement to any situation. We had too much on our plate to try and be babysitting her ass as well. She always into some nigga that we have to keep off her ass. Damn!!!

I looked at June ass stare at this ring, and I felt like something was on his mind, so I asked what's up bro. He just pulled his phone out and through it to me. I read the texts and sat the phone down and then studied his expression. Look you need to reach out to them and see what the hell they want. Don't let this shit bother you. You have made it this long without them, so you don't need them fucking up the life you have made for yourself. Tell Simone your mother is sick and see what she feels. Your sister will be 18 in a few more months, and I don't believe Simone would have a problem with her coming to live with you guys. You can't just leave her like your mother left you. We were boys, and it was hard as hell, but for a girl, it will be twice as hard. You don't want the wrong nigga to get a hold of her.

Now I need to talk to you about this Bolo Situation. I have reached out to a few elites out here who says that this dude is no nonsense. He's a legit business man and is very generous to a lot of organizations across the country, so I'm finding it very hard to believe that he ran off with Rell's money. However you can never be too sure, but we need to be in conversation with this cat real soon.

And that's when we both looked up and noticed Ms. Roberta standing there like she was enjoying our conversation. I looked up and said what's up Ma? She said she was eavesdropping and think that she may be able to help us out. June told her to please sit down because she knows that he don't involve her in any business deals. She laughed as she walked away and said okay. Well, when I go out with my friend tonight I will make sure he knows you guys want to have a sit-down. She closed her room door. Now June and I sat looking at each other like could this get any better?

So apparently Ms. Roberta Ass met this nicca earlier and is meeting up with him for a dinner date. We took care of all the preliminaries and have decided to have a formal dinner party in the suite since we were celebrating and June was going to propose there. Ms. Roberta invited Brian, and we would take it from there. Now don't think for a minute that we are getting soft. This is just a low-key venture, and we weren't trying to make any noise in the streets. After talking to my guys about this Bolo person, he may be a nice business venture, and we all could figure where to put Rell's ass. Now we are never anywhere unprotected, so the suite next door was set up with cameras and our goons were on duty round the clock. We dapped up, texted Charmaine the plans, hired the hotels in–house caterer, and it was now time to get ready.

Simone

God, I love Vegas. All the designers, boutiques, and shopping opportunities keep me smiling. We went to Charmaine friend to get measured for some quick custom dresses that she was going to do for us. She didn't show us the dresses though, but I guess Charmaine already worked that out. We have been out all day, and our driver said that June notified him that we have a dinner party tonight in the suite and to be headed back that way shortly. Now I had bought a few things, but it looked like Charmaine was shopping for two. I may be overthinking it, but I'm not crazy. Anywho, to each his own.

We were now riding back to our suite. Charmaine was going on about how she needed this trip, and I was just happy that June and I were happy. But I remembered that I never checked that message. I would get right on top of that. As we were riding Charmaine was smiling. I asked what she was so giggly for? She said I'm just glad that we can enjoy things like this together. We have weathered the storm, and we deserve it. I must agree. We've had ups, downs, checking bitches, possible murders, drive-bys, robberies, and just generally running for our lives. We stood strong as a unit though. Friends were hard to come by, but Chris and Charmaine were the real deal. I loved Chris just like a brother. He had June's best interest at heart.

I looked up and saw that we were pulling up in front of the hotel and someone from the staff knocked on the window. We let the window down, and he said Ms. Simone and Ms. Charmaine Mr. Savvy asked me to grab your bags and escort you all back to the suite. June's ass had thought of everything on this trip, and I would definitely be thanking his ass later on tonight.

When we got to the suite, my mouth dropped in awe. The dining room was luxuriously set up. It looked like a magazine. I was in awe. I walked over to the table to see a notecard that said this is an all-black affair. Please go to your rooms, get dressed and the dinner party will start at 7:00 pm sharp. See u soon my love. June. I was going up to my room racking my brain to see if I had bought anything black. Then I heard Charmaine scream

Yesssss!!! loudly. I walked to her door to see the Dolce and

Gabanna black mini dress and some black and gold Jimmy

Choo shooties. I laughed and went to my room and boy oh boy

these guys are amazing. I had a long black Jerry McFadden

Chiffon dress that had a split flowing up to the crouch. Some

yellow Lou boutons I had never seen before. But once I noticed

they were signature red bottoms, and I was floored. June went

all out. I looked at the bra and thong set he had neatly laid on

the dresser and saw another notecard with a yellow ribbon. It

read: one last thing baby tie this bow in your hair tonight to set

off your color scheme. I love you. June. God this note smelled

just like him. Polo Red. He knows that Cologne drives me crazy.

Let me get ready. This is turning out to be the perfect night.

June

Ok, everything has arrived. Chris and I are dressed and waiting for our ladies. I was so nervous. What if she says no? I asked Chris, and he laughed and said look, she been waiting for this, so I don't think no is an option. And by the way, after all, u went through to put this Shit together if she says no hell I'll marry your ass. We both laughed, and that made me relax. Chris had a way of knowing what to say to make me feel better.

Finally, I looked up and saw my queen coming down the stairs. Damn!!! That dress is cascading as she walked down the stairs, with an opening leaving nothing to the imagination. What was I afraid of? Why had I waited so long? It's ok, let me keep my cool because It wouldn't be any more time wasted. I cued for the DJ to being softly playing the music we had already pre-selected. Simone was an R Kelly lover, so I definitely had him in the rotation. She smiled as she reached the dining area and said hey boo. We kissed like this was the last kiss. She tasted so good. I pulled back and said girl don't get bent over this damn table. She said press your luck. I smiled tapped that ass and proceeded to kiss Charmaine on the jaw. She was beautiful as well. Chris and I had done well.

Chris popped a bottle of Dom, and we mingled and laughed with each other for a few. Then the door opened. Charmaine's mouth dropped, and she ran over and said, Mommy. Ms. Roberta and her date had arrived. Ms. Roberta said, "hell, did yawl think yawl was coming on vacation without me"? Not! She hugged her momma and mouthed thank you to me. Those two were more like sisters. Ms. Roberta raised Charmaine like a survivor, not a child. That's what made her different. She had so much class but would get them stilettos filthy if need be. She was my Michelle Obama. Crazy, sexy, cool and down for whatever.

We were all laughing and paid very little attention to Brian. Then Ms. Roberta said OMG I got all caught up in this girl and forgot about my boo. Brian smiled like a little church boy. He was dressed to impress though. She made her introductions, and we let the girls be girls while we walked to the den to chat about a little business.

I closed the doors, and we all sat at the table. Brian said, "so you niggas got it like this in the Chi huh? I responded and said ain't no better than how you niggas got Vegas locked right. We all laughed, and now it was time for business. I said let's get down to the reasoning behind us wanting to see you. I mean we know cats all around, but your name came up when we tried to collect on one of our petty loans. This local named Rell in the City owes us 50 g's, and he said that he sent you to take care of that debt and you jumped shipped and came to Vegas with some things left untied. So I'm talking to you to get your side of the deal. Brian looked up at me and laughed. Then he spoke, look I appreciate the courtesy you guys have shown me, and on the strength of Roberta, I came through. Now I've been down in Vegas for six years, and the type of money you are talking about I throw away at the club. Hell, I can pay that off right now, but I ain't trying to right no wrong for some nigga that felt like he needed to add distension in what I'm running. I grew up with Rell and came through the Chi a few weeks ago because he needed some help. Now he needed muscle, and when I got there, his whole operation didn't seem legit, so I bounced. I've come too far to have some local cat from a city I don't even live in bring me down. Now what I can inform you is that the niggas in the Chi' got yawl all fucked up. They think yawl out the game, and the streets are up for the taking. I know that first hand. See Rell told me while I was out there that he was put in a position where he was going to be taking over soon. Some Dominicans that uprooted from Jersey had put him on. That's why he didn't pay your money back because these guys assured him that they were moving in on your territories now that you were businessmen. I told him to look at the whole situation and not just a way to get out, but he assured me he knew what the get down was. I told him that I wanted no parts and that he needed a few lessons in life if he thought it was that easy. Man, I don't even know you guys, but I am aware of the clout you hold in Chicago. It's just business. See every city has to know what toes they are stepping on while traveling.

I looked at him and told him that you are a smart young man. See our positions in the streets are not up for the taking, but we have scaled back only because of the growth of our empire and the expansion of some of our legit businesses. Now those Dominicans, Troy, and Micah are our men. Rell has to be the slowest pack boy in the world to think that we are not aware of what happens in a city that we have had a major part in building. We brought them in because they are grimy and are not afraid of dirty hands. See, we have cleaned our hands and only get dirty if necessary. Chris looked up and said as he lit his cigar, looks like we have to make some noise once we return. I tilted my glass and took the last swish of my drink and said niggas should be tired of the lessons we teaching. We all laughed and continued to talk a little business. It looks like we have just made a new business partner and I was definitely feeling the vibe of this cat.

Ms. Roberta

What? Don't be looking at me like that because my man is looking just as good as yawls. We all laughed. Simone said now momma where did you meet this guy and why is he now meeting with our men? Well, I said, When I first got here I hit the tables in the casino. He kept staring a hole in me until he finally introduced himself. I liked what I saw and what he was talking so now here we are.

When I came back to the suite earlier, I overheard Chris and June talking about this guy from here that they needed to see about some money that he supposedly ran off with and it just happened to be the same guy I met. However, his persona didn't seem like someone that would be running off with petty cash like that. June gave me permission to run the situation by him, and once we realized that he wasn't the true culprit. June wanted to meet him, and since we were going to dinner anyway, June just decided to do something in the suite so we could all enjoy the night together. After giving them my story, I could still feel Simone burning a whole looking at me. What Simone? You already know how I get down girl. I know he's young, but he seems nice, He's definitely packing, and I'm only in Vegas for a little while, and I figured why not have some fun. I need to pay a few bills anyway. We all laughed and noticed the guys coming out of the Den.

Brian smiled at me, and my eyes instantly went to the bulge in his pants. He asked me to show him where the restroom was and I said right this way. We entered my room, and I showed him to the bathroom, and he smiled. I asked what was the smile for and he pulled me closer to him and said this is why I'm smiling. I felt his nature hard and stiff while he hugged me and I looked up and kissed him. He felt my body react to his as his hands explored it. He pulled my dress up and jerked my thong to the side. He stuck his fingers in my wetness, and I gasped in excitement. I could not believe he had my pussy dripping like this. I have had my share of lovers, but damn this felt like I was in my 20's again. I pulled his dick out, and it had to be the prettiest sight I had seen in a while. I pushed him on my bed and whispered that we have to be quick and quiet. He smirked. I leaned over him and proceeded to take him in my mouth. He popped his eyes in gratitude, and he said OMG. Baby you are going to make me cum. I slurped and spit until he was shaking, but I don't do the premature nuts, so I slowed down keeping the same tightness around his member. He pulled me up got off the bed and bent me over. His dick entered me from the behind, and I thought I was a virgin again. My walls surrounded every inch of him, and we both were squealing in ecstasy together. All that kept going through my mind was the fact that I can't fall for this young nigga but then again I could use this in my life. Damn. He said, where you want this nut MA. I said where ever and before I knew it He stroked me deeper and then collapsed on my back as my pussy sucked up all his seeds. Damn! I know we were missed by now. We better hurry clean up and make it back to the party. He kissed me, and we both entered the bathroom to clean up.

June

We were all just sitting around, mingling, eating, and drinking. I am thinking to myself that this is awesome. However, I'm getting anxious. Brian must have had to take a dunk because they been gone a minute. Then again, I know my mother in law, and it's a damn shame that she was probably fucking his brains out. They need to hurry up though before I lose the courage. Just then I heard Chris say welcome back to the party. I looked over and saw Ms. Roberta and Brain had joined us again. I didn't even have any questions. I didn't care. I just needed to do what I planned, and I needed to do it now.

I gave Chris the cue and the time was now. Chris Signaled to the DJ, and he began to play Majors' Why I love you. As the music blasted through the suite, I called for everyone to fill their glasses. I began to tear up as I heard the words to this song play out:

"I found love in you.

And I've learned to love me too.

Never have I felt that I could be all that you see.

It's like our hearts have intertwined into the perfect harmony."

Simone said, "baby are you ok? I said I've never been more ok than I am right now. Look, Simone, I know that you have stuck it out a long time for me. You have waited through some rough patches, infidelities, broken promises and yet right here is where you still stand. I never knew what love was until I experienced you. I have been running from the one person that has always been right there for me. The way you make me feel scares me only because it's a feeling like no other. Like you really have to feel it for you to understand it. Simone said, baby, ok. Don't cry we can talk later after our guest leave. I told her No babe. See our guest are all here just for you. I made this happen for you. The dress you got measured for today is your wedding dress. The trip here is because I'm not running anymore. Today I stand in front of the people that really matter to us and ask you, Ms. Simone Richardson, will you be my forever and a day. My mind of reason, my beauty in the morning, and my queen of the night. Will you be Mrs. June Savvy? As I looked up while I was on my knees, Simone was in awe. She cried so hard that I cried with her. She screamed from the top of her lungs YES. Yes. Yes, and we Kissed like there was no one around but us. She was in love with her ring, and now everyone was in tears. She deserved it. We still got a few things to talk about, but I believe that our love will withstand it all. I'm finally going to be a married man.

Simone

I am just overwhelmed right now. I knew deep down inside that something was going on, but I just couldn't put my mind on what it was. This moment right here is the moment that I have waited for all my life. I love June so much, and I know that we were made for each other. I can't believe my mother kept this from me. We were so close that you would think that we were sisters. But she held her tongue. And Charmaine, my girl, I know she was just happy for me, but she could have told me. I guess they were all in on it. Well, now it doesn't matter because I'm the happiest girl in the world right now. I don't even need a dress. All I need is my man. But I'll let him play this out. He's been very busy in the planning stages. It will all pay off too. I can't wait until we are alone.

This has turned into the best day of my life and I guess from this point on I will start living and becoming the best wife I can be. I know it's going to get hard, but I am up for the challenge. June looks like he just had the weight of the world lifted off of him. In all these years who would have thought big, bad, June would have been worried about losing me. He is a very dangerous man. He is well known in the streets of Chicago, and he is very rough around the edges. But what others didn't know about June is what I did know. He has a big heart. He is definitely what I need, and I'm what he needs.

While he was getting dressed I was finally able to check that message on his phone. Now ok I know you all are like why don't I trust him, oh but I do it's just that sometimes June allow situations to fester, and then I find out when things hit the fan, and then he needs my help. What he didn't know is that there is very little that I don't know. I have known for almost a year that his biological mother was sick. I know that his sister is about to be twelve and she is practically paying all the bills and taking care of their mother. I also know that he sends 6500 a month to take care of the living expenses and his mother's medical expenses. So I know that he said we had some things to discuss, so I'm sure this is one of them. I need him to know these are not his problems. From now on these are OUR problems, and we will manage.

Now he's over there looking at me while I admire this yellow cut diamond, licking his lips. Yep, it's about time to end this dinner party because we got a whole night ahead of us.

Chris

What an eventful time we have had, but now it's time to get back on our grind. When I tell you that Charmaine and Simone can shop, believe me! Now that all is done we gotta get back to business. The wedding was beautiful, the vacation was relaxing, and now it feels great to be home. Charmaine was at the boutique while I was at home digging into some much-needed particulars about this upcoming business venture.

Brian would be leaving Vegas in a few weeks once things are secured. He will be stepping in creating a new tactical squad to hold down the strategic planning of our payroll to the Feds, Cops, and political ties. After becoming familiar with his dealings and actions, we were more than pleased to let him in. We have had him researched and his operations have proven to be worthy.

Now he and Ms. Roberta was a whole different story. See she explained to him that she wasn't looking for no man and he wasn't ready to settle down, so they were just friends with benefits. It was funny though because he gets uncomfortable around anybody that has something to do with her. I don't know what she did to him, but I guess only time would tell.

Once I'm done here, I will be headed over to Junes' because his little sister Amari would be arriving today. 17 years old with a mouth like she thirty. Simone is going to have her work cut out for her. She has been shopping, had one of the guest rooms converted into a palace, and got one of the best schools to accept her in, with a hefty donation I might add. I'm praying all goes well. June isn't so thrilled with the idea, but seeing first-hand what the system can do to you he had no other choice. Sad to say that his mom passed last week and after a small memorial and repass now Amari would be headed to Chicago.

Amari

So Chicago it is I guess. I have been on this plane for about 2 hours and was ready to get off. Now I'm on my way to my new home with my brother June and his new wife, Simone. What June didn't know was that Simone has always kept in contact with me. When my mom first got sick, she came to Miami and introduced herself and kept in contact with me ever since. She had seen the messages I sent on his phone, and because he was so scared of her learning of his past, he never talked about it. I was glad she reached out though. She has been the breath of fresh air that I needed to survive. My mom gave June up at the age of five because she wanted to live her life. I think for that very reason he tries to act as if I don't exist. I had pleaded with him to send for my mom and me when she first got sick, but he was so adamant that I should take care of her like she took care of me. I understand that he was a little bitter, but once she had gotten her life back together, the system had told her that they no longer had him as a ward. By the time she had a private investigator to find him he was in Chicago and had made his life there. Though he wanted to be all tough and hate our mother, he made sure she had the best doctors that money could buy. He also made sure we were well taken care of financially. I was in school, and he refused for me to stop going, so he made sure that she had round the clock care. All of that doesn't matter now. My mom is in a better place, and now I am destined to live out my life in Chicago with my big brother.

Walking through this airport is like a whole new world. I had never been outside of Miami before. I had heard things about Chicago and couldn't wait to get my life going. As I grabbed my luggage this fine man standing in front of me was like, Baby girl what's your name? I said, Amari. He said that I looked like I was lost and was it my first time in The Chi? I answered him and said yes. I noticed he looked older but hell the was nice. And unlike other women, I go for what I want. I would be 18 in a few weeks, and I have never had an issue in the men department. I asked did he live here and he said yep. He said why? Do you need a tour guide? I told him I could use one. He smiled. Then out of nowhere from behind me was this husky voice saying, see that's the shit that's going to get one of these young niggas fucked up. I looked around to see the most handsome brother a girl can have looking down at me with a frown on his face. I said lighten up big bro. Just trying to occupy my time. And then the other voice laughed and said well baby girl you got a lot to learn about these Chicago niggas and I'm offended that you didn't know I was your uncle, Chris. I shook my head and said well don't be offended. I knew who you were when you stepped my way. I am very careful with my surroundings. When I came down to get my bags, I saw June in my peripheral vision and knew you were close by. Now don't get yall panties in a bunch grab my bags and let's hit it. I'm tired as hell, and I could use a shower and some wine right about now.

June

Lord give me the strength to do this! Now out of the kindness of my heart, I am bringing my sister home with my wife and me. I don't want to go to jail, but if she doesn't fix that little attitude of hers, I am going to knock her ass out. Who did she think she was, trying to play us like we were some little chumps. I had to give it to her though; she had us fooled. I noticed how she was able to break down what she saw, and how she saw it playing out though. Let's me know she quick on her feet and she not going to just fall for anything. She definitely has to be on her toes here with me. Simone was so excited about her coming, so I pray to God this works out. Amari would be 18 in a few weeks, and once I see where she is, and how responsible she is, I may spring for her own pad near me. I was paying close attention to her features, and she looks just like my mother. Beautiful, caramel skin, thick in the waist and pretty in the face. I may have bitten off more than I can chew. I have to keep reminding myself of what Simone told me "Baby we can only help guide her as she begins life in a new city, we can't raise her. She is 17 and the raising period has expired. " I just don't want to have to kill nobody. She is young in age, but she built like she twenty-five. These guys are on thirst mode, and I know her little coochie probably hot. I guess we will have a talk once we are settled back at the house. Chris keeps looking at me shaking his damn head. I already know what he is thinking, but I was two steps ahead of his ass. We are going to have to alert my whole team about her arrival as if she was FBI. She is not to be touched or tampered without my knowledge. Oh well, let me buckle up and get ready for this ride. Damn!

Chris

Man, I can see it on Junes face, this transition is going to take the life out of him. Amari is stacked though, and we need to prepare the team because it seems like she is going to be a full-time headache. It may work out for the best though because I am quite sure that Simone and Charmaine will be giving her the ropes, and they will definitely know what's best at this point in her life. We may be overreacting at this point. We are looking at it as if she is a baby and in all actuality, she's not. We got our work cut out for us though.

On our way to Junes, Amari just kept looking out the window and then back to him. You can tell that she had questions but didn't want to ask them. I tried to lighten the mood. I asked what did she like to do outside of school? She answered and said that she was a rebel. We both looked at her with a frown. And she went on to explain herself. She said that her mother really had no rules because during the time that she needed raising she was sick. She also went on to say at the age of fourteen she got into it with some of the local niggas in Miami because they were supplying her mother with drugs. They told her to mind her business. She expressed to them if she found out about them selling to her again there was going to be problems. She says that she had a friend that showed her the ropes, took her to the gun range and kept her on her toes. She said one night when she got home, and her mother was high she went ballistic. She got her piece and scoured the neighborhood for the little punk because that's all he was. She actually saw him with a gang of dudes so she knew she had to play nice. One she got his attention she was able to lure him to the closest motel. She portrayed being interested in giving him some, and he took the bait. He got a room, and they went in. She made sure not to be seen by any cameras because she didn't need any trails leading back to her. She said once in the room he was lighting a blunt and she was making sure she was secured, locked and loaded. Once he was done smoking, she said she looked at him and licked her lips and asked can I call you daddy. The young man then said yeah, come sit on daddy's lap, and she looked at him and smiled. Pushed him back on the bed and straddled him. Once she was secure in him not being able to get up, she reached behind her back and screwed her silencer in and went in for the kill. He thought she was bending down to give him a kiss and she was keeping good on her word and getting rid of her problem. She got up to put her hoodie back on and dashed from the hotel. She heard about the murder maybe days later, but no one ever suspected her, and she never raised an eyebrow, but one thing for sure is that she kept good on her promises.

I told her, look niece, things are not going to be that easy for you here in the Chi. And you don't have to worry about any dirty work anyway because now you got people for whatever you need. But be mindful that this is an operation here, and it's been built on loyalty, honesty, and trust, and we hold strong to those values. We just want you just to enjoy living from now on. She looked out the window, and it looked like I saw a tear, and she said, You right Uncle Chris. I just want to live finally.

June

It took everything in my power not to grab Amari and hold her and never let her go. She was telling me that she had been living like a savage and not growing up. I have yet to understand how she pulled all of these things off and kept a 4.0 GPA in school. No child should have to live like that. I loved my mother. I really did. I mean without her there would be no me. But I just never understood the purpose of having children and not taking care of them. When you become a ward of the state, they have foster parents that are pedophiles, molesters and professional check getters. This is why I got outta that shit the quickest way I knew how. When my mom became pregnant with Amari, she swore she had changed and that she would do right by this child. Evidently, that's not how it panned out. I'm glad baby sis has a few street skills, but I will want her just to enjoy some of the finer things in life. Simone would definitely have a lot to do with that. Yes, of course, we want kids, but we are focused on getting fully legit before that happens. I was a little afraid of the fact that I have to be a full-time big brother now that ready for the challenge. Might not be as bad as I thought to have a little mini-me trying to learn to run this empire. She wasn't any punk either though. She seems like she could handle her own. It's going to be a task getting her to understand that she has people in her corner now. She could just worry about being a young lady and enjoying school, friends, and boys. Well, maybe not so much as boys but you know what I mean. Pulling up to my home I saw it all in her eyes. I looked over, and she said Wow Bro., this is beautiful. My Estate was elaborate and though Chicago was a kick ass city I never lay my head there. I lived in Crown Point, Indiana. Maybe about 30 minutes from the city. I lived in a secure Complex that sits on maybe 15 Acres of land. I have two guest houses. And the main house is where we lived. Seven bedrooms and five full bathrooms. It's quiet, secluded and out of the way. Not many know where Chris and I reside. He's not too far maybe about 20 minutes away in Calumet City. I looked at Amari and told her Welcome home sis. She laughed and said Mi'casa is Su'Casa? I told her hell naw she better get her own. We laughed, and all walked in.

Simone

It's about time yall ass got here. I have been waiting on pins and needles for yall ass all day. June came over and gave me a kiss and said hey honey there is someone that I know you are dying to meet. I looked over at him and said, boy move out the way ......heyyyyy boo. I said to Amari, and she replied by saying what's up Mami'. We hugged so tight. I missed her. June and Chris were looking like they saw ghosts but what time was better than now for them to know that we are not strangers. Amari turned to June and said, ok look, long story short, When momma first got sick Simone reached out to us. She basically raised me and helped me as much as possible to become responsible and to be able to survive at such a young age. June looked at Amari and then to me. I was a little afraid of what he might think. Had I overstepped my boundaries? Had I opened wounds that he just wanted to heal? I then tried to get the weird silence out by speaking. Clearing my throat, I said well, I never meant to go behind your back. June abruptly stopped me and said, please don't apologize. I knew there was a reason you were in my life; you always got my back even when I'm stubborn you are always the voice of reason. I love you baby. He gave me a long kiss that made Chris and Amari both say ....ummm ok, get a room. I looked up from him and told them actually we have several rooms. You all just happen to be standing in one of them. Chris looked over and said, you real funny sis. I told Amari to come on let me show you your room. And let's let the boys be boys. Charmaine will be here soon send her up when she gets here. Amari and I continue up to her Suite. I moved her to the west wing of the main house where there was a family room and two bathrooms in case she wanted to have friends over or something, and they wanted to lounge after school. From the look on her face, she was pleased and probably ready to look in that closet. I had kept her fresh anyway. Whenever I went to see her in Miami, we shopped and she had everything those little girls wished for. So she knew being up here with me and Charmaine she was definitely going to be on point. As we were getting her things put up, I noticed her staring at the photo of her mother I had restored and framed. She rubs the face of the photo and let out a tear. I know deep down she was heartbroken, but we would definitely pull through this. I'm so glad that she can enjoy life now. She had to grow up so early in life. Now she

can learn just to kick back and enjoy life.

Chris

It had been a few weeks since Brian had made his transition and things had been on the up and up. Money was growing, Partnerships on an all time high and life was just good. It was now time to stick it to Rell's ass because the time had been far spent. We had so much going on and literally we had forgotten until June noticed his ass driving around. He spoke to June as if there was nothing to it. Oh well, it's sad when you have to make examples out of people. But with our new growth and money potential, we could not let this go. People needed to know that, if needed, we still made the noise around here. After speaking with June and Brian, we were all meeting up at Bar 10 door in the little Italy area because it was a quiet place on weekdays to do business. Usually, it's only the little after-work drinker and a few other patrons. This place had great food, and that was a plus for us. Brian had also left word for Troy and Micah, our new hittas, to meet us there as well. As I came in, I grab me a glass of Hennesy Privileged. I wanted something smooth today. I saw Brian coming in, and Troy and Micah was not too far behind. We were all just chopping it up when I noticed that it was like 5:20pm. June is never late for a meeting, and this was definitely out of character for him. Actually he usually makes it before me in this type of setting. I grabbed my phone, and I had no missed calls or messages. Then I looked at Brian out the corner of my eyes. It was amazing how we all clicked and was able to be on the same level so quickly. He looked at his phone and gave me a shrug to let me know that he hadn't heard from him either. So I was about to excuse myself from the table when I saw him pulling up outside. He entered, and as usual, the entire place showed him love. Patron Shots all around he shouted as he came to join us. We all dapped and hugged and took our seats. We ordered and was now enjoying our drinks. I looked over and told June, Nigga what's up with you , and why you all smiles today. He said, " man Chris life is just good right now." Brian said really? Well if life is so good right now then why are you like 30 minutes late for this meeting? June looked over and said, That's just it. That's out of the ordinary right? I looked at him and said what's going on June. He said man lately I just been living and smiling. I guess this is just the newlywed in me. We all laughed as he continued to explain how things have been with

Amari being home and how Simone always has his back and how he was going to give them both the world and how By the way Simone is expecting, and you may want to check in with Charmaine because word in my house says that she's expecting too. Hold up, Stop the presses, what did you say? I looked at June, and he had tears in his eyes so I knew this was legit and I'm going to kill Charmaine. Why not tell me? I mean I know that Simone probably knows before me, but damn come to think of it, she has been a little offish lately. Like she told the housekeeper that she needed to get her act together because we don't need any slackers. Then she told our maintenance man that he needed to make sure there was no lead in our home or she was going to put some lead in him. I just thought she was going through a breakdown or something. Ok let me handle this business, and then I will get home. Brian began to let us know what he had figured out along with Troy and Micah. Rell had been doing his part in the streets, but he has slacked in payment because he feels like he is in control now. We got him right where we want him. Slipped all the way up! We let him think that the Killa' Ward was solely run by him. The truth of the matter is that once Brian had solidified his workers, then the plan would be in full motion. We had no need to want Rell even remotely in our business. I know you reading may think that 50 G's is chump change. And honestly to businessmen like us, it is. However, the principle of the matter runs much deeper. It shows loyalty and trust. We had already given Rell part of our city to maintain. He was running short on some investments, and we came through and extended a hand. But don't ever bite the hand that feeds you. I guess this is the message that we will send out. Troy, Micah, and Brian had caught us all up to speed on the plan to murk him. Those soldiers not on board with the plan had already been removed. Now that the plan was put in motion we all finished our drinks, and it was now time to head home. What would I say when I got there. How was I to feel ? I am so happy and nervous at the same time. What type of dad would I be? Emotions just all over the place right now, but it's time to go home and face the music.

Brian

Coming from Vegas was a big step for me. I had made more money than one could count in very little time there. Everything was getting so dreary there. I was losing interest because I had to do everything myself. The soldiers I had were basically just security because I had never trusted anyone. I had made that empire all by myself , but this game is not to be played alone. Though many wish they could, you had to have assistance. So upon meeting June and Chris, we just clicked. Man these dudes have been just like brothers to me. They took me in, and they allowed my input. I decided to come back with them because of the brotherhood. I never had brothers growing up, and from a single parent household, it was always just moms and me. We all kinda have that in common that our moms have made their transition in life and that's a bond that we now share. Loyalty is not always stated but being able to recognize it with them is what set them apart to me. They never stepped to me on no word they heard off the street, they came to me like men and figured it out on their own. That legit shit is what got me because in this business contrary to popular belief it's better to think before you react. Instant reaction could make one come up short.

Now that Rell's ass is history and there is a new team out there I need to just be eyes and ears for a minute. Meanwhile, I have been just laid up with my boo for a few days. Come on now did you think that I wasn't still tapping Ms. Roberta's ass!!! That's gonna always to be mine. She can bitch and moan about not wanting to be tied down, but as long as I'm paying the bills, laying this pipe, and keeping her kept, she gonna always be mine.

Charmaine

I don't know who was more nervous, Chris or myself. We had talked about this for years but for it to become a reality was unbelievable. It's so funny because he and June had turned into military sergeants. Simone and I couldn't do anything. It was a wonder we could shit on our own. I guess the plus would be that the sex was amazing. Now I'm trying to learn to get adjusted to being home because it's getting close to our due dates. Simone was due in two more weeks, and my due date was a week after that. I had done everything I possibly could to get things together. My hospital bag was ready; The nursery was almost ready. It just needed a theme. We decided not to learn the sex of the baby, so we had brought everything that's needed , We just would have the contractors finish the nursery once the baby is born. Simone had called and told me that Amari had been a great help to her and June. She has gotten used to living with them and has become a great lil sister. Also, June has purchased a building that is currently being constructed into a roller rink. He is going to let Amari become the sole proprietor. She is going to be so ecstatic. It has a roller rink, Snack area and party area with a Humongous Studio DJ booth. He wants her to own this so that the Young adults have something more to do than standing around outside and end up statistics. Amari can add her own flare once it's established. Things have just all around been great for all of us. There have been a few hiccups here and there, but we move in silence, so we have things back under control. Brian has taken over most of the hands on and has built a street team that is far beyond anything imaginable.

Simone

Being pregnant did not mean that we were not still fly. June is a pest. Everything I wear is too tight, my heels too high, too much cleavage showing, to much ass showing. OMG, I really wish he would give it a rest. Now that he and Chris have gone out of town, its time for me to take care of some business. Since finding out that I was pregnant, I haven't really worked much. Amari and a few of her friends were running my beauty supply stores, and Moonie had been running most of my private clients and anything he needed we would work trough fax and email. My secretary , Tish could have easily done the job , but she was abruptly fired. June said that she was a part of spring cleaning and I never knew what happened. I just figured he trusted Moonie more until Amari told me what had been going on. Apparently, since I was allowing June to run the operations at his request, she felt that she needed to get a little closer to the boss. She began to throw passes at him, and he warned her that he would let her go. Now the funny thing is that she knew a little bit more about our businesses than desired because I had grown to trust her. But bitches hated when they were not you. I never understood why hoes felt like they should have what you have. I worked for this shit. This isn't any fly by night shit, we built this shit together, and some hoe with a desire to have and not a passion for work was not going to infiltrate on me. June did the right thing, but I can't let this slide without making an example. She knew too much, and I needed leverage, and I had it. I needed to let her know this game is for real and Tricks are for kids.

 Amari, Charmaine, and I were off to the mall. I got word that Tish was now doing makeup for MAC at River Oaks Mall. As we made our way through the mall, all eyes were on us as usual. We didn't even look like we were almost due to have these babies. However pregnant or not we were still fly. We arrived at Macy's and our plan was now in motion. Amari went ahead of us to the Mac counter, as we just browsed through some of the new fashions. Eventually, we all ended up there. Tish looks amazed to see me and yelled as if we were old girlfriends. She tried small talk, but Charmaine cut to the Chase she asked when was her break and she said she could leave now. So we all headed to the food court to catch up. Now we were not crazy with all the cameras in every inch of this Mall however when we needed to make promises we did!! We sat in the food court, and I looked at her and cut to the chase. I asked her to take a look at this picture. It was a photo of her Son and me at his daycare that she thought no one knew about. She looked at me with tears in her eyes. Amari came behind her and spoke in a tone a little above whispering. Look if you want to make sure he has a great life and you want to continue to live yours, you better forget that you ever met June and Simone Savvy. Is that understood? She looked up and said, yes! and went on to say that she was sorry. I asked, What are you sorry for? She said for trying to sleep with June. She went on to let me know that he instantly fired her and told her never to think that she had it that sweet. I laughed and said oh! this visit has nothing to do with that. This is just a reminder that once you no longer work for me, you no longer know me. She shook her head and said she understood and went back to work. See that's what's wrong with female these days. She honestly thought that I would threaten the life of her son over a Man. Naw I'm from the old school, if a nigga goes then he wasn't mine in the first place. She had seen so much information in working for me that I was making sure that my clients information remained confidential. I had faith in June and knew that he would do the right thing. I was just making sure that I could continue to secure my bag! Though most clients are dealing with me were legit, and if It wasn't I handled on my own, I just had to always make sure things were covered.

June

Hey babe, I said to Simone as she wobbled through the door. Empty handed I might add. As she retired on the chaise, I asked her, what did you buy from River Oaks today? She looked astonished and said, what are you talking about? And I thought you were out of town anyway? Now after all these years of knowing me, Simone should know that being pregnant with my very first seed, that I have tabs on every move she makes. No insecurities of course, but we're not angels so I must protect my family at all times. I sat next to her and took off her shoes and began to rub her feet. She looked up and laughed and said one day I'm going to give your little security detail a run for they money. Stop having me followed everywhere. I'm a big girl, and I can handle my on. FYI, I didn't go alone anyway. Yes, I know. You took my sister hot head ass and pregnant Charmaine with you. Somebody gonna kick yall wanna be tough ass. She looked like she wanted to be mad at me, but I wanted to fuck, so I was going to let her down easy. Just let me handle things baby please? She was enjoying her foot rub, so she could only moan an answer. Hearing that moan turned my ass on. I put her feet down and bent that ass over the Chaise and went to work. I loved her so much. This pussy was wet as hell too. I loved this pregnant pussy. It seemed like it just automatically made my dick hard. As I continued to stroke that ass from behind I felt my veins about to burst. Between her yelling and my reaching total ecstasy, I had no Idea that her water broke. As I pulled out, I noticed that she was still leaking and she said, baby, I think my water broke. OMG. I was a wreck. I told her to stay there. I went to the bathroom and got a towel to wipe her clean . I remained calm. I noticed a few speckles of blood upon wiping her down, but I didn't wanna alarm her. I got her hospital bag, and we headed for the hospital. She looks scared, but contractions were only 13 minutes apart. We will be there in no time. I am overly excited. Everyone has been notified and are on their way to the hospital. Amari is getting Ms. Roberta who acts like she is having this baby and not Simone. We here baby, let me get a Wheelchair. With tears in her eyes, she said hurry babes. Before I could get to a wheelchair, Ms. Roberta was rushing out with a chair talking about move out her way. I laughed as I tried to remain calm, but I was so damn excited. It's finally happening. I had so many emotions running through my mind. We got up to labor and delivery, and the doctor said they needed to do a C-section because the baby was breech. I instantly though we had done something wrong. I broke down like never before. I didn't want to hear anything. But everyone was assuring me that this was normal. I went to a corner and chilled. I saw Brian walk over. He said look June I know how you feel, been there done that. It's gonna happen man . Now go in and support ya girl she must be a wreck by now. He was right . I was so selfish for a moment that I didn't even think about Simone. Let me get in this room. By the time I got down the hall nurses were running everywhere. Sir, you have to stay here. All I could remember was that. I heard nothing else. Finally, Chris came and grabbed me and sat me down. He said everything is going to be alright bro. They said Simones' Blood pressure was high so they needed to sedate her to calm her down. The baby is fine. They will do the C-section as soon as she wakes and can keep the pressure normal. I broke down. I cried on his shoulder like never before.   He took me for a walk down the corridor and made sure nobody bothered me. We got to a little corner room, and there was solitude. I needed it. Upon getting a few moments of silence, I noticed Chris looked worried too. I needed to pull it together cause we would be right back here for him in a few weeks. Everybody is different, so I don't want him to think that Charmaine is going to have problems too. I looked over and heard a knock on the door, and it was Troy and Micah. These two never went anywhere without the other. Before I could answer, Chris said he don't want to be bothered right now. Troy said look man both of yall could grab ya panties out yo ass and get out here. Simone is going into surgery now and umm Chris you can go downstairs because I guess with all that's going on Charmaine's ass decided to be in labor too. She is in the ER. He looked . We hugged, and both went off to be the fathers we were destined to be.

Chris

Look at us. So I guess I can catch yall up. June and Simone had a very healthy 7lb 3oz baby girl named Christina Briana Savvy. And Charmaine had given birth to a beautiful baby girl Juneesha Brean'Jones which was 9lbs 4oz. We both wanted to include Brian in our kids' names because he couldn't have children. He had made himself Uncle of the year already. We were all leaving the hospital, and he drove up with a van full of customized items for the girls. I said, Brian, what is all this? He said that he had a hook up with the owner of Baby Room Couture. They specialize in all this custom stuff, and he didn't know what to buy, so he brought everything. These babies were going to be spoiled beyond measure. Troy and Micah came around to the front of the hospital with the trucks to escort us all home. Brian and Ms. Roberta were in the van already. June looked over and gave me the eye as we both noticed a white Taurus, tinted windows sitting there with the passenger window cracked. Now we didn't have any beef recently, so it was just a little off beat for us. Anyway the car sped off, and we just let those negative thoughts fly. We had been in a good place and was trying to remain there at least until the girls were settled in

and used to being mothers. Truth being told our wives were

lethal and we couldn't risk their safety anymore. This was going

to be a hard pill for them to swallow but we would have this

conversation with them real soon.

Ms. Roberta

Life is good right now. My first grandchild is so fat, cute and spoiled. She is a mess already. Things have slowly gotten back on track, and I have been reluctant to tell Brian about this car that I think has been following me. Now it appears everywhere I go but never home because I have routes that are unheard of when it comes to home. However when I was at a book club reading the other day on the Southside, and I saw a white Taurus outside of the venue. I really didn't pay it any mind until when I left the window area, it moved as well. When I left the book reading, I went to I-57 to pick up Brian some turkey tips and there it was again. Maybe I was paranoid but I damn sure ain't no fool. This has been going on for about a week. Now I know you all are thinking like why would I keep risking it. Now listen, in this family that we have built there are no punks, and I try to keep light work for myself. Now if they wanted led up they ass then they would step to me. I have been running these streets for a long time, and I am quite aware when your target is unreachable you come for what's close, near, and dear. Now, do you think that I would be out on these streets with no training? I was waiting to lay a motherfucker down. Now even though I wanted to be Queen Bee and shit, I had a conscience. I just didn't want the family to get back to business as usual yet. But my gut was telling me that I needed Brian to know what was going on.

Brian

I was just walking in and noticed Roberta sitting in the corner of the room. It wasn't unusual for her to be in solitude but I just had an eerie feeling about what was going on with her. She had called, but I was in a meeting with the DA handling some business matters. As I walked over, she looked back and said: " I need to talk to you, Brian." I was in shock. We kind of just flowed together. Never really had any heart to heart conversations. Just an automatic attraction that made us seem as if we just fit. I listened as she explained what had been going on and I was instantly irritated. Here I am in charge of the security detail, and I can't keep her safe. She tried to calm me down, and I became furious. I asked why she just now mentioned it and she said that she wasn't scared, but she thought that I should know in case something happened. Well, nothing was going to happen on my watch. She so damn hard headed but she is going to have to stay put for a minute until I figure this out. I sat across from her in deep thought until she looked startled and said 'Babes the car is in front of the house". I did an all call page, made her go to her room and darkened the room so that I could look closer. As I continued to watch, I noticed that the car engine had been turned off. I couldn't see inside the car because the windows were tinted. Who the hell sends somebody in a damn Taurus anyway? And now there was someone approaching the front gate. Oh, so you want to face trouble head on right. No Problem. Made sure I was locked and loaded and buzzed the gate without even asking who it was. Told Roberta to stay put, but as usual, her ass was right behind me. I wasn't worried though my baby was a ridah'. As this man approached the door, I opened it. He raised his hands and said ummm is Roberta here. I put my pistol down and looked her way. From the look on her face, I knew she wasn't surprised to see this dude. She looked up and said, Greg? He said yes. He went on to say," I thought that was you I saw a few weeks ago, but I have been apprehensive to approach you didn't know what your situation was." He looked at me and said you must be her son, I'm Greg, an old Friend. I looked at this cat and laughed and said. No. I'm not her son , I'm her man, and it's a little late for company. Maybe you can come catch up another time. He looked stunned and said oh ok. Well, Roberta, it's good to know that you are ok. Have a nice night. And you have a nice life I said and turned to her with fury. She tried to walk off, and I grabbed her and turned her around before I could question her Troy, Micah, June and Chris was beating the door down. I decided to have this conversation with her later. I explained what was happening to them and they all seemed to think this was all funny. Not funny to me. June went on to tell me how Greg and Ms. Roberta used to have a thang, but he couldn't handle her attitude. Well, I guess she forgot to mention this Greg character to me. I mean its cool. We know what it is with us. When they all left after chopping it up for a minute, I sat in silence. Was I jealous? I think I was. I couldn't imagine her being with someone else. Is he why she didn't want to be tied down? I guess it's time for us to face a little reality.

Ms. Roberta

I can't even believe this shit. All this time this has been Greg ass following me. I had a right to let Brian shoot his ass. He would come back after all these years. In a damn Taurus at that. I don't need any problems in my life right now. What people didn't know is that dealing with Greg was a constant problem. He was needy, and he was very abusive. Had I let June know that when we were together, his ass would have already been floating up a damn river somewhere. He thought he could come into my world and live, eat and sleep off me because he had a bomb with his tongue. I really hated the person I was with him. He was good for appearance and just to be involved with somebody, but he was not even on my caliber. I hated him and everything that he stood for. I know why his ass is coming around now and that's because he wants something. It's cool though because now that I know I will deaden this issue on my own. I couldn't help but feel my pussy tingle when Brian was like he was my man. I know I had told him I didn't want to be tied down but that was to protect my heart in case one of these ratchet ass hood rats caught his attention. I will definitely talk to him, but I need to handle this situation first. I would usually call Simone, but I need to handle this on my own and June not going to kick my ass for putting her in danger. I got this on my own, and then I will talk to my boo and see what we can work out. I would hate to lose him over this bullshit. As a matter of fact let me go in here and assure him that this pussy is his.

Brian

Well, I guess my boo was feeling some type of way. She came out that back room and asked no questions. She began to stroke her hand over my shaft, and I instantly stood at attention. Something about her that I always just instantly got in the mood. No matter what she had done or what was said. It was just that type of connection. That irritated me because here I am supposed to be angry, and she got me aroused like a motherfucker. I let her seduce me because I knew what she was up to all along. She just needed me to know that pussy is still mine. After she had swallowed my seeds, I was damn near about to fall out. She came and wiped me off and kissed me and said that she would be back. She had to run an errand. I told her ok. And to be careful. I wasn't thinking straight. I was looking up at the ceiling thinking about that head she had just given me. That shit was the bomb. She was like the best I ever had when it came to that. Now back to reality. Where the hell did she think she was going this late at night. I instantly grew jealous once more. Made a few calls and headed my ass out the door. She thought shit was sweet out here. I had her car on GPS because we decided a long time ago that we would keep these women safe. I pulled up the info and headed to where she was. No why in the hell is she in the heart of the Englewood. I sat still for a moment until I noticed this damn white Taurus again. Now let me get this straight, she sucks the hell outta my dick, says nothing about this nigga but yet leaves home to meet this motherfucker. I will have to calm down. But I am going to this place. I know she is in this warehouse because it's the only thing on this block. As I slipped up the side walkway, I heard voices. I could hear them arguing. I heard the male voice saying " now you think you tough cause you running with these street niggas. I will make you suck that pistol Roberta" I tried to keep my composure and listen to what she said. " Greg I will never let you back in my world. And running with street niggas don't make me tough, I was born and branded for this. Now when I was with you, it was only for show because the minute you started putting your hand on me I knew your days were numbered anyway. I just came to give you common courtesy and explain why you about to take your last breath" I couldn't let her do this thought. I didn't want to risk that the wrong person may have seen her. I kicked the door open and Splat. All his brains were on a wall right beside me. She looked at me and put the gun down. When she looked at me, we always shared a silent language. She left and got in my car. Troy and Micah had made it now. Micah took care of the inside, and Troy took her car back home for me. We rode in silence, and I saw a tear fall from her eye. She wiped it and then said. Look, Brian, I love you and don't want to lose you. I didn't want to commit because I thought you would find someone younger and leave me. I love the way you make me feel, the way you smell, the way you make love to me. Everything about you just screams I need you in my life. " I listened to her and just said. Roberta, I love you too and I'm not going anywhere. We will figure this whole relationship thing out. Don't worry. We rode home and I knew when I got there we would be fucking like Jackrabbits. I couldn't wait.

Troy and Micah

Though you haven't really heard much from us, we play a big part in this empire. We are twin brothers born and raised in the Boogie Down Bronx. June and Chris sent for us after a heist we controlled at LaGuardia Airport. We have been doing their manhandling every since. Those guys brought us in and treated us like royalty. I mean we come from grit, so we were not new to organized operations. Making and keeping families safe and organizations run clean was our specialty. When they brought Brian in, he was like an uncle to us. He not only handed out orders on the streets , but the brother had life lessons and a lot of knowledge for us. Now, do we believe in Karma? Hell yeah, we believe in that bitch. We know it's coming! We just have a good eye to catch it before it gets there. We have been dodging that bitch for years. She'll hit us hard. My only suggestion is that she come like a beast because anything else will be an easy defeat.

Sincerely,

Troy and Micah AKA The Twin Towers

Brian

This transition has definitely been the best decision I have made in my life. I have gained two brothers and two beautiful Sister-in-laws. One very unique niece and two beautiful, great nieces of whom I happen to be godfather to. Though every story can't be told, and every mishap can't be relived, we have definitely put in work. I'm not proud of every life decision, but I am very happy to be able to say that past mistakes were worth my present situation. Business is good. Bank accounts are fat. And My woman is the baddest cougar a man can ask for. Don't get it twisted, I worked hard for my stake in this and with all the work I put in the fruits of my labor is gravy. So until next time remember that life has its ups and downs and you choose your own road. Do I believe in Karma? Hell yeah. So since tomorrow is not promised I live each day as if it's my last.

Sincerely,

Brian AKA Bolo

CDO of Savvy Enterprise

Amari

Well, look how life has a way of turning itself around. I was born to a drug-addicted mother who had given up my brother of whom I had never known about until later in life. My mom wasn't the best but because she kept me I felt obligated to stay. Coming up sleeping around for my next meal and a roof over our heads was my life as a kid. When she became sick, I felt obligated. I never understood why my brother would not come and rescue us. He told me to come a long time ago, but I couldn't leave her. He did step in financially but would never come. His wife did though, and for that, to her, I am ever indebted. Since the passing of my mother, I have learned how to become the woman I needed to be. I have gained a beautiful relationship with my brother, and we often talk about my mom now which makes me happy that he's even remotely interested in who she was as a person. I own my own skating rink and club right now, and I am finishing up my business degree at Columbia College. Our empire has left blood on a lot of our hands but when you can break free and have a normal life full of the things you always wanted is much satisfaction for previous struggles. Now do I believe in Karma? No. I believe in living my life to the fullest. I tackle obstacles as they come and I don't classify them with things I've done in the past. You may feel different, but I guess we all will see.

Sincerely ,

Amari Renae Savvy

Ms. Roberta

I am at a place in life where I live like there is no tomorrow. Life is great. I have a beautiful new granddaughter and a God-granddaughter. I treat them both the same. They are adorable and definitely know they can get anything from grannie. I have a beautiful home. Noticed I didn't say house because that's what I used to have. Now that Brain and I have made a commitment to each other it has become a home. He is so attentive to me, and it's sad that I had to wait so late in life to experience this type of love from someone half my age. However, I love him, and he loves me. We enjoy each other and the lives we live. I'm still a little reckless, but my grandbabies have slowed me down. Where do I stand in the family business? Right smack in the middle. I do what needs to be done and have no regrets. Now do I believe in Karma? Fuck that bitch. I don't got long to live anyway.

Sincerely,

Ms. Roberta Richardson

Charmaine

This has definitely been a whirlwind of years for me. I have gone from that thuggish little hustler as a teenager to an astounding young woman. I have the man of everybody's dream in my corner. My husband is the epitome of a real man. My daughter has raised us both. Time goes by so fast. I am my husband's ride or die. He starts a sentence, and I finish it. What we have built together no one will take apart. It has been a long journey, but life as we know it is great. We still move in silence but with a lot more consideration than before. Deals and connections will always be a part of our lives we just have a lot more to think about than usual. We have definitely made great strides for the life that we live, and I will take nothing back. We have endured a lot of hurt and a lot of grief. Through it all, it has made me a better Wife, mother, woman, and overall a better person. Do I believe in Karma? I don't even know what Karma is. Things happen for a reason, and that is if you live your life looking for it to spiral downward, it will. Until next time.

Sincerely,

Charmaine Jacobs

Simone

What a series of events over these last few years. I have been hustling since my teenage years, but now I can breathe. Went back to school, my own accounting firm, four beauty supply stores, two real estate management firms, a very handsome and devoted husband, a beautiful baby girl, and a sister in law that seems like she is my blood sister. I don't know what you think about me, but I pray all the time. Conviction eats at my soul, but I live the life I chose. I believe God covers those that want covering. Repentance is a part of my daily life. I wake up daily grateful because I am aware that the very breath that I breathe is undeserved. Do I believe in Karma? Yes. What goes around comes around right? Am I looking forward to it? Hell no, but it won't be unexpected. I just have to get my house in order so that when it comes, it won't hit heavy. Thanks for walking this journey with me and I'm sure you will hear from me soon.

Sincerely,

Simone Richardson-Savvy

Chris

Oh, what webs we weave. When you are born, and you learn how to discover things, language, behavior, and energy surrounding you it develops your character. Though you can change the route of your life and the person you have become, you can never adjust your character. That's what's embedded in you from birth. You can hide it but, never change it. I learned that trust is earned from an early age. I met June and trust and loyalty was instantly instilled. We are partners in this thing. The crazy thing is that there are no I's in team. We have built an empire, and together we enjoy a life full of things that once seemed unimaginable. We both hold degrees in our prospective areas of business. Our wives are educated as well. We all just came from nothing and made something. Is this a story that people would mimic their lives to, I hope not. We grimy, gutter , ass niccas. We live and die by the sword. Do I believe in Karma? No. What I believe is that punks jump up to get beat down. If you want it, come get it. Don't worry, because I'll be waiting.

Sincerely,

Christopher Jacobs CFO of Savvy Enterprise

June

Fatherhood had really made me a better person. Coming from a broken home encouraged me to do better. My daughter wouldn't have to wonder where her next meal was coming from. She was growing so big, so fast and I loved every single moment. Simone was a beautiful working mother. Even though we had nannies in place, Christina knew exactly who she was. She spent every free moment with her. Caring for her, caressing her and you already know she is dressing her. It has definitely made our bond stronger. We have been trough some trying times, but we have stood together and endured. They say to choose your wife wisely, and I say choose the one who you can't imagine life without. The one that compliments your very being. The one who knows your past, and still stands with you at your present, looking forward to your future. That's what I have. I have come a long way . I am not proud of some of the things in my past, but I'm intrigued that I had a plan. Hustling is not a lifestyle. It's a stepping stool that some seem to get stuck on. I learned a long time ago that what seems sweet eventually turns sour. You can be the best at every move you make in the game and no matter where you turn someone is trying to knock you down. The people in my very small circle were hand-picked. They were tested and tried, and loyalty among thieves always reigned supreme. This thing is bigger than just me. It's a network of like-minded individuals. Though I started this, believe me, we all eat. Do I believe in Karma? Let me think about that for a moment. It's like cause and effect. The intent and actions of an individual influence the future of that individual. So does this mean that Karma is all bad? I don't believe so. See I have done a lot of dirt in my life and I have also done a hell of a lot of good. So my waves seem to balance themselves out. Does that mean I won't hit a pitfall? Not really it just means that I'm June and my very existence is not for me but for the family coming up behind mean. I am afraid of nothing but God. So until I meet my maker, I live.

Sincerely,

June Savvy CEO of Savvy Enterprise